That's Not a Fish!

An Ivy and Mack story

Written by Rebecca Colby

Illustrated by Gustavo Mazali

with Camilla Galindo

Collins

Who and what is in this story?

Listen and say

aquarium

Ivy

Mina

Download the audio at www.collins.co.uk/839686

Mr Hill

🎧 Ivy and Mina's class went on a school trip to the aquarium. Mina said, "I love fish. I've got some fish at home."

Ivy said, "I love fish too. I *eat* them at home." The girls laughed.

"Try and find everything on your papers," their teacher, Mr Hill, said.

The aquarium was very big. Ivy and Mina looked through the glass.

"What a beautiful pink fish!" said Mina.

"That's not a fish!" said Ivy.

Mina and Ivy read about the jellyfish.

"You're right. It's not a fish," Mina said. She looked at the paper. "But it is on here."

"Fantastic!" said Ivy, and ticked the jellyfish on her paper. "Let's find the starfish next."

The girls looked for a starfish.
"Look!" said Ivy. "I'm a starfish."
Mina laughed.

Mina read, "A starfish is not a fish!"

"Are there *any fish* to find?" asked Ivy.

"I don't know," said Mina. "The next animal is a turtle. Is that a fish?"

"No, I don't think it is," said Ivy.

Ivy and Mina looked at the turtles.
"They are NOT fish!" they said.

"Where are the fish?" asked Mina.

Ivy saw a boat. "Quick, Mina," she said. "Let's find some fish."

"Quick, Mina. Get dressed in this suit. We can swim in the sea," said Ivy.

Mina laughed again. "OK," she said.

"Let's get into the water," said Ivy.

"It's nice in the water," said Ivy.
"Come and swim with me, Mina."

Ivy and Mina were in the sea. They looked for a fish.

Ivy saw a sea animal. She swam to it. "That's not a fish," she said.

'But these are," said Mina.

'Hooray!" said Ivy. "Lots of fish!"

The girls swam on. Ivy pointed at some seahorses. "These are *not* fish!" she said. "Look at their tails!"

"Yes, they are," said Mina. "Seahorses *are* fish, Ivy."

"Oh," said Ivy. "I'm sorry, seahorses! You are fish."

Ivy and Mina saw an old boat. There were lots of beautiful fish here.

And some ugly fish, too. They saw a big brown and blue fish.

"You are a very big fish," said Ivy.

"The biggest fish!" said Mina.

"No," said Ivy. "Look! I think that's the biggest fish." A shark swam next to the window of the boat.

"Let's go back," said Mina.

"Yes, let's go back," said Ivy.

Mr Hill came over to Ivy and Mina.

"Did you find everything?" he asked.

The girls smiled. "Yes, we saw everything."

"Well done, girls!" said Mr Hill.
"Let's have lunch."

In the café, Ivy said, "We did great work finding fish."

"And we did great work *not* finding fish," said Mina.

Ivy smiled again. "Look! We have fish for lunch."

Mina saw her sandwich and said, "Now, that is a fish!"

"... or is it?" they said, and laughed.

Picture dictionary

Listen and repeat

aquarium

jellyfish

seahorse

shark

starfish

turtle

1 Look and order the story

2 Listen and say

Collins

Published by Collins
An imprint of HarperCollins*Publishers*
Westerhill Road
Bishopbriggs
Glasgow
G64 2QT

HarperCollins*Publishers*
1st Floor, Watermarque Building
Ringsend Road
Dublin 4
Ireland

William Collins' dream of knowledge for all began with the publication of his first book in 1819.

A self-educated mill worker, he not only enriched millions of lives, but also founded a flourishing publishing house. Today, staying true to this spirit, Collins books are packed with inspiration, innovation and practical expertise. They place you at the centre of a world of possibility and give you exactly what you need to explore it.

© HarperCollins*Publishers* Limited 2020

10 9 8 7 6 5 4 3 2

ISBN 978-0-00-839686-2

Collins® and COBUILD® are registered trademarks of HarperCollins*Publishers* Limited

www.collins.co.uk/elt

British Library Cataloguing in Publication Data

A catalogue record for this publication is available from the British Library.

Author: Rebecca Colby
Lead illustrator: Gustavo Mazali (Beehive)
Copy illustrator: Camilla Galindo (Beehive)
Series editor: Rebecca Adlard
Publishing manager: Lisa Todd
Product managers: Jennifer Hall and Caroline Green
In-house editor: Alma Puts Keren
Project manager: Emily Hooton
Editor: Deborah Friedland
Proofreaders: Natalie Murray and Michael Lamb
Cover designer: Kevin Robbins
Typesetter: 2Hoots Publishing Services Ltd
Audio produced by id audio, London
Reading guide author: Julie Penn
Production controller: Rachel Weaver
Printed and bound by: GPS Group, Slovenia

MIX
Paper from
responsible sources

FSC
www.fsc.org

FSC™ C007454

This book is produced from independently certified FSC™ paper to ensure responsible forest management.

For more information visit: **www.harpercollins.co.uk/green**

Download the audio for this book and a reading guide for parents and teachers at www.collins.co.uk/839686